Small in the City

Sydney Smith

WALKER BOOKS
AND SUBSIDIARIES
LONDON • BOSTON • SYDNEY • AUCKLAND

First published in the UK 2019 by Walker Books Ltd
87 Vauxhall Walk, London SE11 5HJ

This edition published 2020

2 4 6 8 10 9 7 5 3 1

Text and illustrations © 2019 Sydney Smith

First published in the United States 2019 by Neal Porter Books, Holiday House Publishing, Inc.
Published by arrangement with Holiday House Books

Printed in China

British Library Cataloguing in Publication Data: a catalogue record for this book is available from the British Library

ISBN 978-1-4063-9298-2

www.walker.co.uk

This book is dedicated to the memory of Sheila Barry.

I know what it's like
to be small
in the city.

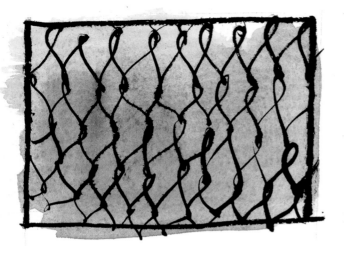

People don't see
you and loud
sounds can
scare you,

and knowing
what to do is
hard sometimes.

Taxis honk their horns.

Sirens come and go
in every direction.

Construction sites pound
and drill and yell and dig.

The streets are always busy.

It can make your brain feel like
there's too much stuff in it.

But I know you.
You'll be all right.
If you want, I can give you
some advice.

Alleys can be good shortcuts.

But don't go down this alley.
It's too dark.

Three big dogs chase and
bite each other in this yard.
I would avoid the place ...

if I were you.

There are lots of
good places to hide,
like under this mulberry bush.

Or up the black walnut tree.

There is a dryer vent that
breathes out hot steam that smells
like summer.

You could curl up
below it and have a nap.

The fishmongers down the street
are nice.

They would probably give you
a fish if you asked.

This empty plot looks like a
good place to rest, but the bushes
have burrs.

They might get stuck
to your coat.

I know you like to listen to music.

In the blue house down the street
someone's always playing piano,
and there is a choir that
practises in the red brick church.

You could perch on the window ledge.

In the park I have a favourite bench.
Sometimes my friend is there.

If you see her, say hi.
You could sit on her lap
and she will pet you.

But home is safe and quiet.

Your bowl is full and your blanket is warm.

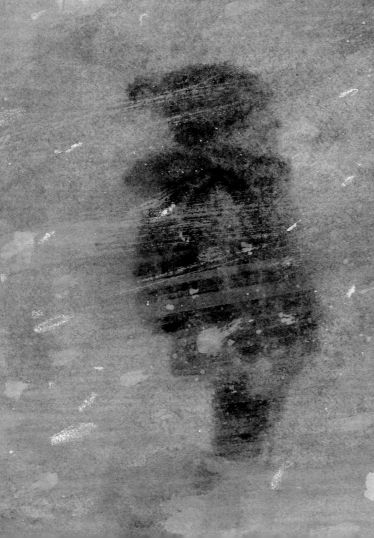

If you want,
you could just come back.

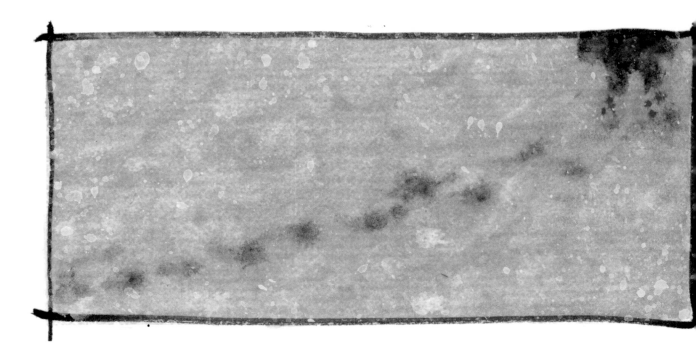

But I know you.

You will be all right.